# NATURALLY ME

Written By

Maricia Duhart

# NATURALLY ME

Published by: Joseph's Ministry, LLC

www.josephsministryllc.com


Ordering Information:
Quantity sales. special discounts are available on
quantity purchases by corporations,
associations, and others. For details, contact the address above.

First Edition
Copyright © December 2021 Maricia Duhart
ISBN- 978-1-953928-29-0

I thank God for inspiring me to write this book and for placing Josh Debolt, CEO and Cofounder of Sociallutions Media Group in my path. I dedicate this book to my daughter Imani Patterson, and my granddaughter Blakely Duhart-Wilkins. Always put God first and he will exceed your possibilities. Imani no matter what curve balls life throws your way, I will always be your number one cheerleader.

"God has plans for you." Jeremiah 29:11

-Maricia Duhart

When I look and see myself in the mirror,
I see a beautiful brown girl looking back
at me with afro puffs and curlies,

I'm naturally me.

You are my sister, and I love your afro puffs and curlies. When I look into the mirror, I see a cocoa skinned beauty with straight and curly hair with a gap in between my teeth.

I'm naturally me.

Hello, you two queen. When I look into the mirror, I see my apricot skin with straight blonde hair, and I too appreciate me,
CHEE

I'm naturally me.

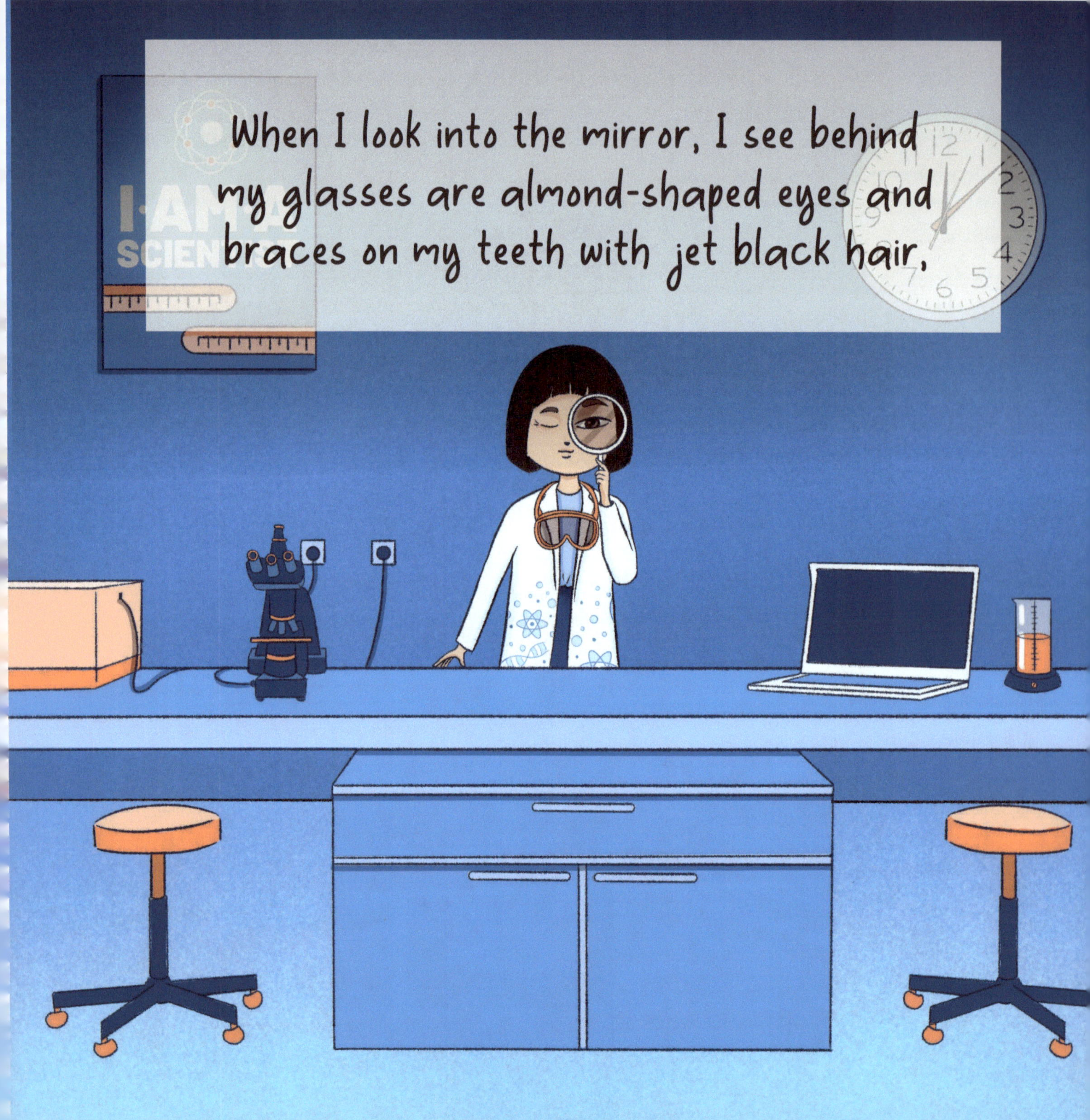
When I look into the mirror, I see behind my glasses are almond-shaped eyes and braces on my teeth with jet black hair,

I'm naturally me.

When I look into the mirror, I see a girl with locs the color of brown and blonde, with a red tint to my skin and a band around my head that some may think is tin,

I'm naturally me.

When I look into the mirror, I see my heritage from ancestors to me with high cheekbones and two long braids, not to forget to mention a feather in my hair. I've also been taught not to stare,

I'm naturally me.

When I look into the mirror, I see a girl with straight black hair covered with a hijab and a dot in between my brow,

I'm naturally me.

When I look into the mirror, I see a girl
with a pink laced cap, an apron dress,
and clogs on my feet,

I'm naturally me.

When we look into the mirror, what we see
are all different girls who are unique; from
the color of our skin to the shoes on our feet,

We are naturally me.

THE END

My name is Maricia Duhart. I grew up as a military child and spent my adolescent years in Germany. I had the opportunity to travel to different countries in Europe. I was also blessed to have a diverse group of friends from the schools I attended, with while living overseas. I wish for every young girl to embrace and love every being of themselves.

*"When you look into the mirror always see the beauty in you!"*